The Frog Who Couldn't Ribbit

The story of
The Frog Who Couldn't Ribbit
and all the pictures in this book are
original and have been specially
commissioned for Tesco.

Published by
Tesco Stores Limited
Created by Brilliant Books Ltd
84-86 Regent Street
London W1B 5RR

First published 2000
ISBN 1-84221-127-7

Text © 2000 Rod Baber
Illustrations © 2000 Brilliant Books Ltd
Printed by Printer Trento S.r.l., Italy
Reproduction by Colourpath, England

1 3 5 7 9 10 8 6 4 2

fun to learn

collection

The Frog Who Couldn't Ribbit

Illustrated by
Anne Wilson

Written by
Rod Baber

Once upon a time,
not so very long ago, there
lived a frog in Greendom,
called Rupert. Now Rupert was
a very unhappy frog because,
unlike all his frog friends,
he could not ribbit.

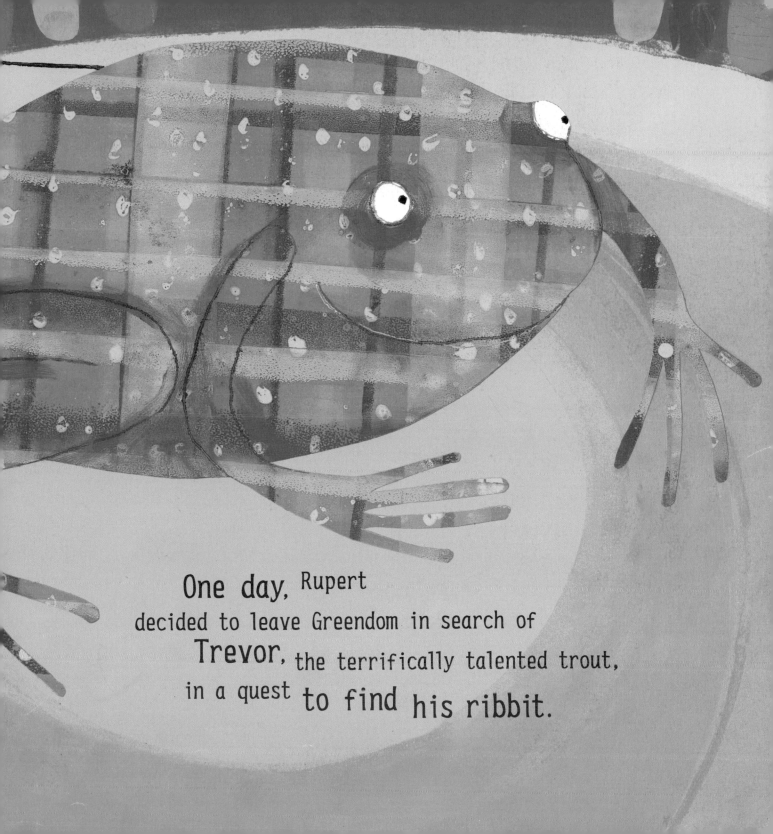

One day, Rupert
decided to leave Greendom in search of
Trevor, the terrifically talented trout,
in a quest to find his ribbit.

The distance would be far –

over the Lumputty River

and Marsh Mellow Mountains

and then across the Pongo Plains –

but Rupert's spirit was so strong
that nothing could sway him from his path.

After a full day's hopping,
Rupert arrived at the Hip Hop Café
on the edge of the Lumputty River.

It was where all the **hippest, hoppest
frogs** hung out. Rupert coolly hopped up
to the counter and **asked** the groggiest
frog how to cross the river.

All the other frogs stared at Rupert.
Some even knocked over their glasses of frog grog –
they knew that only a **few foolish** frogs
had **ever dared** to cross the river,
and none had **ever** returned...

'My little green one,' croaked the groggiest frog,
'the only way across is on Oscar, the odd otter.
But if you don't amuse him, he'll gobble
you up – he has a taste for little frogs.'

Rupert wasn't put off. He gulped his fly juice
and **hopped down** to the river's edge.
Oscar, the odd otter, slimed towards him and
smiled a slithery smile. 'Do you want a ride?'
'Oh, yes please,' said Rupert, bravely.
'Then jump on,' the smiling otter said.

The little frog jumped on to the otter's tummy and they started to swim across the river. In the middle, the otter stopped. 'Entertain me or I'll eat you up, from your wet, webbed feet to your glistening, green ears,' he snarled.

'OK, you smelly, wet,
    stinky, odious otter –
watch this!' Rupert yelled.

Then, using his biggest hop of all time,

   he parachuted over to the other side

of the river, leaving Oscar snarling far behind.

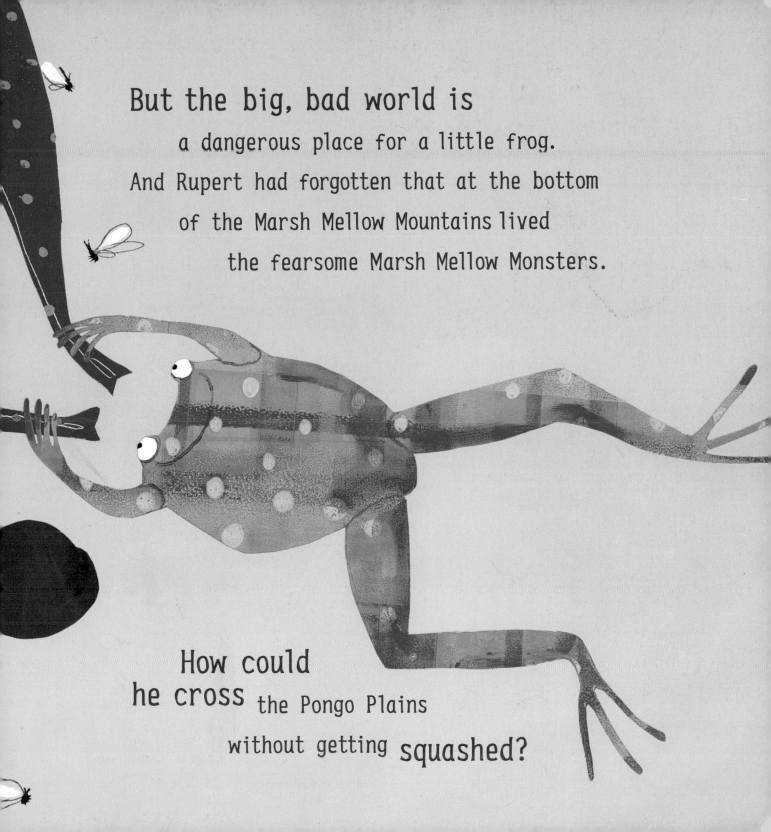

But the big, bad world is
a dangerous place for a little frog.
And Rupert had forgotten that at the bottom
of the Marsh Mellow Mountains lived
the fearsome Marsh Mellow Monsters.

How could
he cross the Pongo Plains
without getting squashed?

Then he remembered – Marsh Mellow Monsters love marvellous melons!

If he could only find a melon marvellous enough, he was sure he could count on their help!

Soon he found what he was looking for.

A melon so moist and marvellous no monster could resist it.

At the first monster he came to,
Rupert nervously cleared his throat.
'Excuse me, Mr Monster,' he said politely.
'Would you let me cross the Pongo Plains
in exchange for this truly
marvellous melon.'

The monster
scratched its hairy head,
it rolled its roving eyes.
'All right,' it said, scooping Rupert
up in its paw, and carrying him
right across the Pongo Plains to
the edge of the Pongo Pond.

'Does Trevor,
the terrifically talented trout,
live here?' asked Rupert.
'Yes,' said the monster, 'but he'll
only appear if he thinks your
question deserves a reply.'
'OK!' said Rupert, lowering his mouth
to the pond. 'It's Rupert, the frog,
here,' he said, 'please can
you make me ribbit...?'

Rupert waited... and waited...
His little frog heart sank to his
webbed feet. Perhaps Trevor wasn't going
to **answer** him. Downheartedly, he turned
to head for home. But... just as he did so,
he heard Trevor, the trout,
bubbling to the surface!

'Why do you want to ribbit?' huffed the fish.

'Because I want to be an average, straight-down-the-line, normal frog,' Rupert replied.

'Normal is boring,' puffed Trevor. 'But I'll grant your wish. But... you must swear not to ribbit for twelve whole frog months.'

'OK,' said Rupert.

Then Trevor gave Rupert two small
jars of reinforcing ribbit-replacement
jungle juice and Rupert drank them down.
'Don't forget your promise,'
said Trevor, as Rupert thanked him
and hopped off for home.

The **Marsh Mellow Monster** helped him back across the river. And at last – tired and exhausted – **Rupert** arrived back **home**.
He told his friends all about his **amazing adventure** and when he had finished, not one of the other frogs asked if they could hear **his new** ribbit.

Rupert kept his promise, and for twelve whole frog months not **a ribbit** passed his lips. He thought he understood what Trevor had meant.

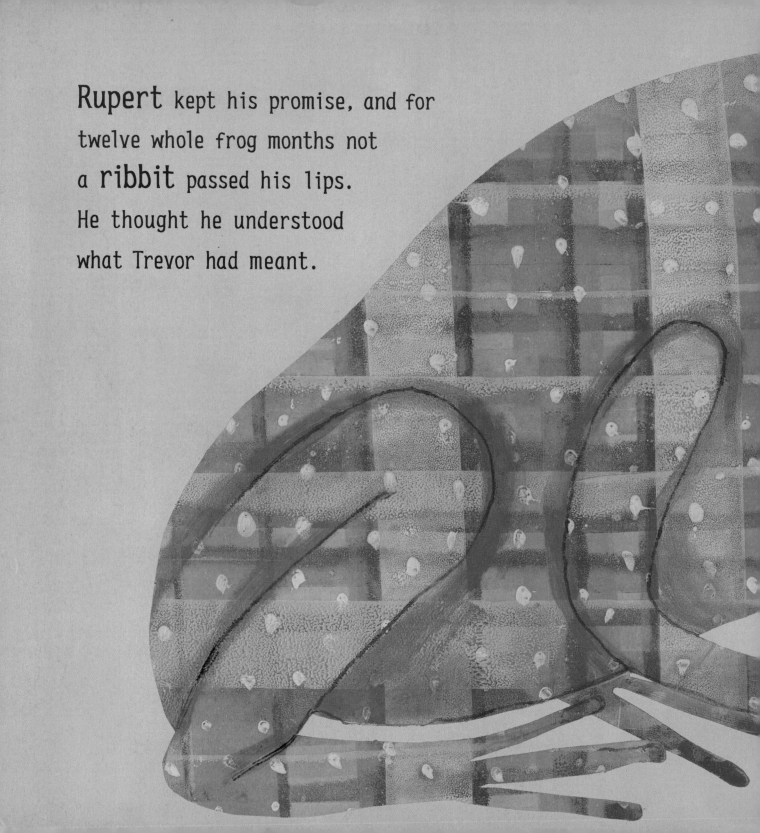

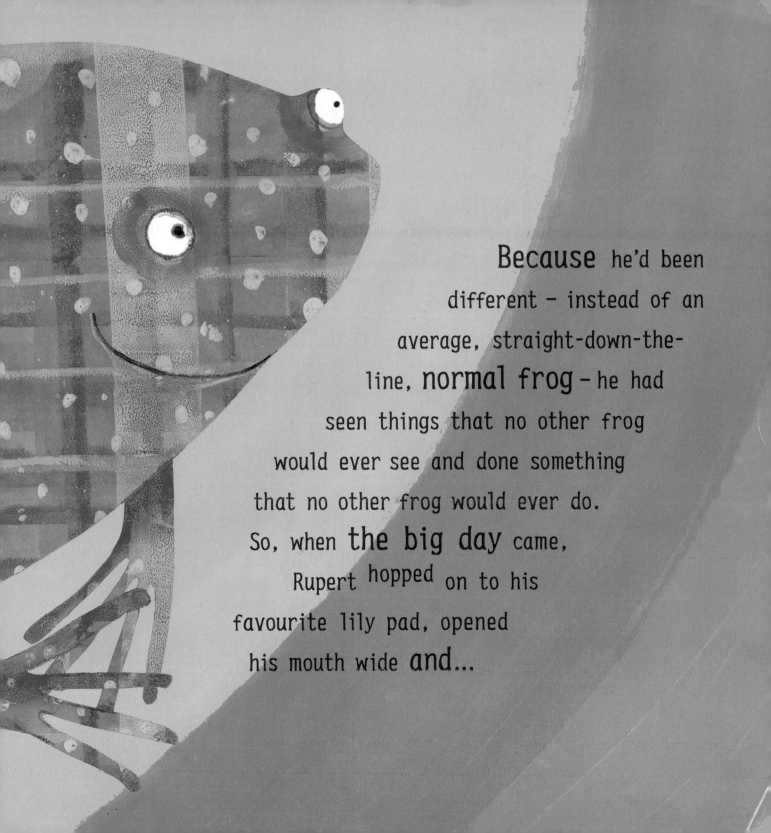

Because he'd been different – instead of an average, straight-down-the-line, **normal frog** – he had seen things that no other frog would ever see and done something that no other frog would ever do. So, when **the big day** came, Rupert hopped on to his favourite lily pad, opened his mouth wide **and...**

...didn't make a sound!
He liked being different, he liked being
the frog who couldn't ribbit,
he liked being him –
just the way he was.

And do you know what?
So did everyone else!